THE FENWAY
FOUL-UP

BALLPARK
Mysteries 1

THE FENWAY
FOUL-UP

by David A. Kelly
illustrated by Mark Meyers

A STEPPING STONE BOOK™
Random House 🏠 New York

*To my parents, Kevin and Nancy, who show
rather than tell when it comes to life.
—D.A.K.*

To Kasidy—thanks for being my muse. —M.M.

*"I don't want to play golf. When I hit a ball,
I want someone else to go chase it."
—Rogers Hornsby*

Text copyright © 2011 by David A. Kelly
Illustrations copyright © 2011 by Mark Meyers

Published in the United States by Random House Children's Books, a division of Random House, Inc., New York.

Random House and the colophon are registered trademarks and A Stepping Stone Book and the colophon are trademarks of Random House, Inc.

Visit us on the Web!
SteppingStonesBooks.com
www.randomhouse.com/kids

Educators and librarians, for a variety of teaching tools, visit us at
www.randomhouse.com/teachers

Library of Congress Cataloging-in-Publication Data
Kelly, David A.
The Fenway foul-up / by David A. Kelly ; illustrated by Mark Meyers. — 1st ed.
p. cm. — (Ballpark mysteries ; #1)
"A Stepping Stone Book."
Summary: Cousins Mike and Kate are at Boston's Fenway Park when the Red Sox's star hitter discovers that his lucky baseball bat has been stolen.
ISBN 978-0-375-86703-3 (trade) — ISBN 978-0-375-96703-0 (lib. bdg.) —
ISBN 978-0-375-89816-7 (ebook)   4861 3920 6/12
[1. Baseball—Fiction. 2. Stealing—Fiction. 3. Cousins—Fiction. 4. Fenway Park (Boston, Mass.)—Fiction. 5. Mystery and detective stories.] I. Meyers, Mark, ill. II. Title.
PZ7.K2934Fe 2011   [Fic]—dc22   2010008521

Printed in the United States of America
10 9 8 7 6

Contents

The Green Monster

"Watch out!" Kate yelled.

Boston's best batter, Big D, had just hit another rocket. The baseball was headed straight to the top of Fenway Park's left-field wall, right where Kate Hopkins and her cousin Mike Walsh were standing.

"Yowza!" Mike ducked down as the ball sailed overhead. "That one is out of here!"

Mike and Kate watched it fly over the wall of the stadium toward the sunny city street below. They waited to hear the clunk of the ball hitting a car's hood. Or shattering glass as it hit a windshield.

But all they heard was a loud *thud* and a soft *thunk*. No crunch. No smash of glass. No car alarms.

Mike scampered up to the railing that overlooked the street. The ball bounced against the wall of a parking garage. A little girl in yellow overalls chased the ball as it rolled down the sidewalk.

"Aww . . . why didn't it land near us?" Mike asked. He pulled a worn tennis ball out of his fleece jacket and bounced it against the cement steps a few times. He carried a ball everywhere he went. "I've always wanted a real major-league baseball."

"If Big D had hit it at you, it would have knocked your head off," Kate answered. She took off her baseball cap and slipped her long brown ponytail through the hole in the back of the cap. "At least then you wouldn't be able to think about baseball. It's all you do."

Mike couldn't argue with that. He did spend a lot of time playing baseball. And talking about it. And watching it. Last year he even started a baseball website. That was why he was so excited to be at Fenway Park, watching batting practice.

Kate's mom, Mrs. Hopkins, worked as a sports reporter for a popular website, American Sportz. She was covering that day's baseball game between the Boston Red Sox and the Oakland A's.

Kate lived with her mom in Cooperstown, New York. Mike lived down the block. His mom and Kate's mom were sisters.

Mike, Kate, and Kate's mom had left at seven that morning and driven to Boston. Mrs. Hopkins was in the pressroom, but Mike and Kate were using their special "All Access" passes to explore Fenway Park. They had started at the seats on top of Fenway's giant left-field wall. The thirty-seven-foot-high wall was painted dark green and ran from left field to center field. It was known as the Green Monster.

Mike turned his attention back to the field. "Hey, watch the way Big D stands in the batter's box." Mike pointed to home plate. "He has an open stance. His back foot is closer to the plate than his front foot. It's what gives him power to hit like that."

Even from far away, Big D's arm muscles stood out through his uniform. He was tall and strong and always had a big grin on his face. Big D was one of Boston's most popular players.

"Do you see the bat he's using?" Mike went on. It was a light-colored wooden bat with a dark green ring dividing the handle from the barrel of the bat. "It's his good-luck charm, like a four-leaf clover. He calls it his Green Monster—just like the wall."

Pow! Big D hit another ball out of the park. Across the field by the Boston dugout, a small group of fans cheered. They had come early for batting practice, too.

"Didn't he try to use a bright green bat in a game once?" Kate asked. "What happened to it?"

Mike was the expert when it came to baseball. But Kate knew a lot about everything else. She read all the time—books, newspapers, websites, anything she could find.

"Yup, but it wasn't allowed," Mike told her. "According to the rules, bats have to be black, brown, or natural. So now Big D just uses a regular bat. But he still calls it the Green Monster."

After he batted, Big D headed back to the dugout. The fans crowded the railing and chanted, "Big D, Big D, Big D!"

Big D leaned his bat against the low wall in front of the seats. He took off his hat and waved. The fans went wild. Many of them held out baseballs, hats, and other souvenirs for Big D.

Big D started signing autographs. A photographer trailed behind him, taking pictures. He carried a long black tripod case slung over his shoulder and a camera with a big lens.

"I knew we should have waited over

there," Mike said. "We could have gotten Big D's autograph."

"Maybe next time," Kate said. "It's cool that he's signing so many."

While Big D greeted the fans, Wally, the Red Sox's big furry green mascot, came trotting down the first-base line toward home plate. He waved to the people near the dugout, but then he tripped and sprawled face-first on the grass.

The crowd roared with laughter while Wally wriggled on the ground. Big D and a batboy ran over to help Wally up. Wally took a small bow and gave the crowd a big wave—without falling over.

Big D patted Wally on the back and ducked into the dugout.

One Red Sox player after another practiced hitting. But Mike and Kate could tell that no one was as good as Big D. Soon, Boston finished batting practice. A batboy and batgirl came out to collect the bats.

"I'd love that job," said Mike. "You'd get to

meet all the players, watch the games, and get paid for it!"

The Oakland A's took the field for their batting practice.

"Come on," said Kate. "I told my mom we'd stop by the pressroom before the game starts. She's going to give us some money for lunch."

Kate and Mike found their way through the hallways lined with hot dog, ice cream, and peanut stands. They rode an elevator up to the fourth floor. After showing a security guard their passes, they entered the pressroom. The room had huge open windows facing the infield.

"Hi, kids," Mrs. Hopkins said. She was sitting at a desk in front of a window. A few reporters sat on either side of her, working on computers or talking.

Mike went straight to the windows. "Wow! What a view," he said. "You can see everything from here. It's like you're on top of the field!"

"It *is* pretty amazing," said Mrs. Hopkins. "Sometimes foul balls get hit up here, so you have to pay attention."

Just then, a telephone rang. Kate's mother reached for it. But the reporter next to her answered it. He talked for a minute or so, and then hung up.

"You'll never believe what just happened," he said.

"What?" Mrs. Hopkins asked.

"Big D's lucky bat has been stolen!"

The Batboy

"Stolen?" Mike asked.

"Yes," the reporter said. "It's been his favorite bat ever since he hit his four hundredth home run with it."

"But we saw him with it just a little while ago," Kate said.

"The security chief thinks someone took it after Red Sox batting practice," said the reporter. "Big D was doing a TV interview in the locker room. Usually the batboy or batgirl

11

picks up the bats after practice. But they couldn't find Big D's."

"It's probably worth a million dollars," said Mike.

The reporter laughed. "Maybe not a million," he said. "But I'm sure a private collector would pay an awful lot for it."

A loud *CRACK* ripped through the ballpark. One of the players had hit a line drive. The ball flew straight into center field.

Mike turned to watch where it landed. A flash of blue caught his eye. "Hey, the police are down near the Boston dugout. Looks like they're questioning that batboy," he said. "I bet *he* stole the bat."

The batboy was talking to two people dressed in blue. Mike could make out the word SECURITY on the back of their shirts.

"Oh, that's just Bobby the batboy. He's a

nice kid," the reporter said. "I doubt he stole Big D's bat."

"The ballpark security people are probably just interviewing witnesses," Kate's mom added. "I'm sure they'll also check equipment bags and lockers for the bat."

"I saw that batboy with all the bats earlier," Mike said. "He seems kinda suspicious to me."

"You think everyone's suspicious, Mike," said Kate. "But I still want to see what's going on. Can we check it out, Mom?"

"Sure. Your seats are next to the dugout. I've got to stay here to work on my column." Mrs. Hopkins handed Kate a twenty-dollar bill. "Don't let Mike spend it all on souvenirs," she joked.

Kate pocketed the money. As they were about to leave, the pressroom door opened and a man walked in.

It was the photographer from batting practice. He had his camera bag and tripod case slung over his shoulder. A water bottle poked out of one of the big pockets in his jacket.

"Just dropping off my tripod," the photographer said. "You're lucky you don't have to lug all this gear around."

He dropped the camera bag and tripod case to the carpet with a grunt. Then he rummaged around in one of his jacket pockets and pulled out a bag of sunflower seeds. He poured a few of the black and tan seeds into his mouth.

Mrs. Hopkins smiled. "Try lugging a computer, some reference books, and a pile of research papers around! That's not easy, either," she said.

"I guess everybody thinks their job is hard," said the man. "It sure would be nice to be rich. Maybe I'll win the lottery soon."

The photographer slid the long black

tripod case under a table and poured himself a cup of coffee.

Mike turned to watch the batboy talk to a security guard. The second security guard searched the sides of the field and the box where the photographers sat. Kate gave Mike's arm a tug and pulled him toward the door.

"Thanks for the money, Mom," Kate said. "We'll catch you after the game."

Ten minutes later, Mike and Kate were sitting in their seats, eating hot dogs and popcorn. They were only a few rows away from the Boston dugout. On the field, the Oakland A's were still taking batting practice.

"Awesome seats, Kate!" Mike said. "Your mom got great tickets. I owe her a few car washes."

"Great idea," said Kate. "She'd love that."

Swish! The Oakland player at the plate swung and missed.

"Hey, there's the batboy," said Mike. He shaded his eyes against the April sun and pointed at the dugout. "Doesn't he seem a little old?"

The batboy wore a bright white Red Sox uniform and a baseball cap pulled low over his forehead. He kept glancing back over his shoulder and scanning the stands.

"I read that you have to be at least fourteen to be a major-league batboy. He looks older," Kate said.

She motioned for Mike to lean in close to her. "He does seem a little shifty," she whispered. "Think we should try to ask him a few questions and see what he does?"

"Always thinking like a reporter, aren't you?" said Mike.

"Well, *you* said he looked old," Kate replied.

"I may be suspicious, but you're nosy," Mike teased.

"I'm not," Kate said. "I just like to know what's going on."

She fished around in her popcorn for the most buttery pieces. Finding one, she popped it into her mouth. "What do you say?" Kate asked. She dug through the popcorn for another buttery piece. "Should we go talk to him?"

"Uh, I don't know," said Mike. "It seems like he might want to talk to *us* instead."

Kate looked up from her popcorn. The batboy was staring straight at them!

For a moment, Kate was startled. Then she relaxed. She shook her head. "Actually, I think he's watching that guy in front of us," she said. "And I can see why. Doesn't the guy know that the Yankees are Boston's biggest rivals?"

The white-haired man sitting in front of Kate and Mike wore a New York Yankees baseball cap.

"But he's also wearing a Red Sox shirt," Mike said. "I guess he's confused. Or maybe he just likes both teams."

Out on the mound, one of Oakland's coaches wound up and threw a fastball.

The batter swung at the pitch. *POW!* The ball flew into left field. Even the coach turned around to watch it. *TONK!* The ball bounced off the Green Monster.

"Awesome hit," Mike said. "In any other ballpark that would have been a home run, but not here. You have to hit them really high to get over the Green Monster."

"Yeah, it was a nice hit, but he's not as good as Big D," Kate said. "Big D blasted it over the Green Monster twice in batting practice."

"But that was with his lucky bat," Mike pointed out. "Who knows how he'll hit without it. I bet if he doesn't find it, the Red Sox will lose today's game!"

Sunflower Seeds

"Look, Kate, the batboy is gone. Let's check out the scene of the crime," Mike said. He stood up.

"You can't go down there," Kate said. "It's probably against the rules." Kate wasn't afraid to do something risky, but she needed a good reason. She didn't like getting in trouble.

"Even if it is against the rules," said Mike, "they'll probably just tell us to go back to our seats."

Mike started to edge through the row of seats toward the aisle. As he was walking, his elbow clipped the man in the Yankees cap.

"Hey, watch what you're doing, kid!" the man said. He had taken off his hat and was rubbing his head. "You should be more careful. Now I've spilled my sunflower seeds."

Mike looked down. The ground near the man's feet was covered with little black and tan seeds.

Kate shook her head and rolled her eyes. Mike was kind of clumsy.

Mike turned red. "Oh gosh, I'm sorry," he said. "I can get you another bag if you want."

The man held up a white and red bag. "That's okay," he said. "There's plenty left. Just try to keep your elbows to yourself from now on."

"Sure," said Mike. "I'm really sorry."

The man put his Yankees cap back on. He tucked the bag of seeds into his pocket and started kicking the spilled sunflower seeds away.

Kate and Mike had reached the aisle when there was a whooshing sound followed by a loud *clunk*.

They whirled around to see the man pick up a long white plastic tube from the ground. On the side it said BIG D LIFE-SIZE POSTER. He must have knocked it over with his foot.

The man set the poster tube against his armrest. Then he noticed Kate and Mike watching him.

"I'm fine," he said, shooing them away. "You can move along." He frowned and examined the poster tube carefully. There was a dark smudge halfway up the tube. He rubbed it with his sleeve.

Kate grabbed Mike's arm and pulled him down to the infield railing. It was almost game time. The seats and aisles were starting to get crowded with fans.

"I feel bad about bumping into that guy,"

Mike said. "Did you see how worried he was that he knocked that tube over?"

"Maybe he's embarrassed," said Kate. "You don't like it when people see you do something dumb, do you?"

"Actually, I wouldn't know," Mike said. "I never do anything dumb!"

"Oh yeah? What do you call bashing that poor man with your elbow? A smart move?" Kate teased.

Mike rubbed his elbow for a second. Kate was right—he was always knocking into things. His arms and legs sometimes seemed longer than he remembered.

"I can't help it if his head was in the wrong place," said Mike.

With one final line drive, batting practice ended. The players went back to their clubhouses to get ready for the game.

"Hey, Mike," Kate said, "what's that?"

Just over the railing in front of them, specks of black and tan lay scattered on the red infield dirt. They were right where Big D had put his bat before it was stolen. Mike leaned over the railing to get a better look.

After a minute, he straightened back up.

"Sunflower seeds!" he said.

Kate glanced over her shoulder at the man with the Yankees hat. He was reading a Red Sox program.

"Do you think *he* took the bat?" Kate asked.

"Well, he's eating sunflower seeds. And he was here for batting practice," Mike said. "I'd say he's a prime suspect."

"If he took it, he must have given it to someone already. He certainly doesn't have the bat now," Kate said.

"Maybe," said Mike. "Or maybe he hid it

behind the dugout or under the seats."

Out on the field, the umpire brushed off home plate. Fans streamed into their seats around the ballpark, carrying hot dogs, drinks, and popcorn.

Mike felt a tap on his shoulder. He whirled around. It was an usher.

"Do you two have tickets?" the usher asked in a gravelly voice.

Kate handed their tickets to him. "We're sitting over there. We were just trying to see if the batboy would give us a used ball."

Kate was good at thinking on her feet. When she needed to, she could come up with a reason for just about anything. It was a handy skill for keeping out of trouble.

The usher looked at the tickets and then gave them back. "You can stay here for now. But make sure you return to your seats when the game starts," he said. "You may not have heard, but Big D's lucky bat is missing. We're asking all the fans to keep an eye out for any strange activities."

"Okay," Kate and Mike said.

The usher moved on. He asked the other nearby fans for their tickets as well.

On the sidelines, a few players started to stretch. Suddenly, Mike leaned way over the railing.

"What are you doing?" Kate said. "Are you crazy? You'd better watch it or you're going to fall onto the field. We might get kicked out!"

"Just . . . getting . . . a . . . sunflower . . . seeeeeeeeed . . . ," Mike huffed. He stretched his right arm as far over the railing as he could.

"Hey, kid, cut that out! No one's allowed near the field during a game!"

Mike quickly straightened up. The batboy towered over him. The batboy had caught him red-handed.

"Fans aren't allowed to reach over the railing or touch the field," the batboy went on. "You could get in a lot of trouble if anyone else saw you."

"Sorry," Mike said. "I guess I got carried away."

"We heard about Big D's missing bat. We were just looking for clues," Kate jumped in. "Do you know anything about who took it?"

The batboy tilted his head and squinted at them. He pushed his Red Sox cap up. "I might," he said. "But why should I tell you?"

Mike and Kate exchanged a glance, then Kate shrugged.

"My name's Kate Hopkins, and this is my cousin Mike Walsh. My mom's a reporter for American Sportz. She's up there in the pressroom." Kate pointed to the window above them.

The batboy's face lit up when he heard the name American Sportz. "I love your mom's articles," he said. "My name's Bob, but they call me Bobby Batboy around here. It must be cool to travel to all the ballparks and write about different baseball teams," Bobby added.

"Mom likes it," Kate said, "but Mike here would rather have your job."

"It's fun," Bobby said, "but it's a lot of work."

Bobby looked thoughtful for a second. "Can you guys keep a secret?" he asked at last.

Instantly, both Kate and Mike said, "Yes!"

"Good," Bobby said. He lowered his voice. "The security team found a ransom note at one of the souvenir stands about half an hour ago. The note said that if Big D doesn't pay by the end of the week, his lucky bat will end up as firewood!"

Bobby glanced over their shoulders. He leaned in toward Kate and Mike. "See the man in the Yankees cap back there? He was one of the fans standing near the dugout during batting practice," he whispered. "He was close enough to take the bat. The security people are investigating."

"I knew it!" Mike shouted. He gave Kate a high five.

The batboy looked puzzled. He frowned slightly. "Knew what?" he asked.

"He was our top suspect, too," Mike said. "Because of his sunflower seeds."

"That's what Mike was trying to get when you caught us," Kate explained. She pointed to the pile of black and tan shells near the wall.

"Wow," said Bobby. "Sunflower seeds! Right where the bat was stolen! I'd better go tell security. Thanks for the tip."

The Secret Code

The grounds crew hustled to get the field ready for the game. They wore matching red polo shirts and tan shorts. One man bent down and sprayed white paint on home plate. Another did the same for the small strip of rubber on the pitching mound.

"So Bobby thinks the man in the Yankees cap stole the bat," Kate said. "Do you think they have enough evidence to arrest him?"

"Not unless they find Big D's bat," said Mike.

Kate leaned against the railing. A man dressed in khaki pants and a dark jacket was walking along the warning track next to the Green Monster. Out of nowhere, he opened a green door in the wall and stepped through it.

"Did you see that?" Kate asked Mike.

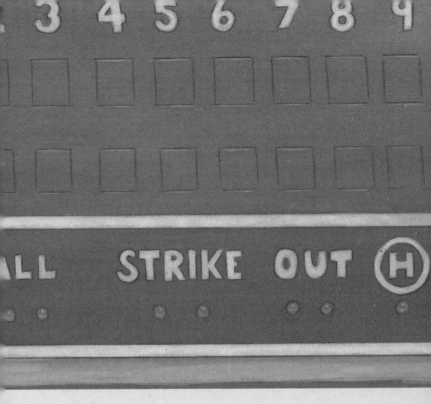

"There's a hidden door in the outfield wall! How cool is that?"

"That door's used by the people who work the scoreboard," Mike said. "Most parks have electronic scoreboards, but Fenway's is old-fashioned. They change the score by hand."

Fenway's scoreboard was about half the

height of the Green Monster. It was painted green to match. White lines that ran from top to bottom divided it into sections.

The lines reminded Mike of something he had read a little while ago. "What if the bat is hidden somewhere really obvious," he said, "just like Fenway's hidden message?"

"What hidden message?" Kate asked. She loved puzzles.

"It's on the scoreboard," Mike told her. "It's easy to see once you know about it."

Kate's forehead wrinkled as she squinted to study the scoreboard. She saw places for each team's score and red and green lights to record balls and strikes and outs. But no hidden message.

"I give up," said Kate. *"¿Dónde está?"*

"Come on, Kate," Mike complained. "Not more Spanish!"

Kate was teaching herself Spanish. She liked to challenge Mike with new words and phrases.

"Okay, okay," Kate said. "Where is it?"

"If you give up that easy, we'll never find the bat," Mike said with a smile. "It's in the white lines going up and down on the right side of the board. They're not solid stripes. They're dots and dashes. Know what that means?"

"Duh!" Kate said with a flip of her ponytail. "It's Morse code. I should have seen that! Morse code uses dots and dashes to spell out letters—like SOS is dot-dot-dot, dash-dash-dash, dot-dot-dot."

"Bingo!" said Mike.

"Let's see, I guess I'd read it left to right, top to bottom. Dash, dot-dash, dash-dot-dash-dash. That should be TAY."

"Wow, that's right," said Mike. "You know a lot of weird stuff, but Morse code? How'd you learn that?"

Kate looked down and blushed. "After my parents got divorced, my father used to write me coded messages," she explained. "When he'd send me or Mom a letter or e-mail, he'd put part of it in Morse code for me to figure out. And I'd write him back in Morse code. It was fun. After a while, I got good at it."

"Pretty cool. I never knew that," Mike said. "It'll come in handy if you ever want to be a telegraph operator!"

"Ha-ha, very funny," said Kate. "What's Morse code doing on the scoreboard in Fenway Park?"

"It spells out TAY and JRY. Those are the initials of Tom Austin Yawkey and his wife, Jean Remington Yawkey," said Mike. "They used to own the team. They hid their initials on the scoreboard for fun."

"I never would have noticed it if I wasn't looking for it," said Kate.

"Those dots and dashes got me thinking. What if the bat is hidden in plain sight, like the initials or the door?" Mike asked. "What if the thief used the bat as . . . as a broom handle or something? Or maybe the thief put it in a backpack or an umbrella."

"It wouldn't fit into a backpack. It would have to be in something longer," Kate said. "But you're right, the thief could have stashed it somewhere around here."

They looked around. None of the fans nearby had coats or umbrellas with them. One man had a long crutch and a bandaged leg, but the crutch was too narrow to hold a bat. They checked, but the bat wasn't hidden

under any of the seats around them or by the Red Sox dugout.

"Hey, what about the man in the Yankees hat?" asked Kate. "Remember the poster tube that he kicked over? Maybe he stole the bat and hid it in the tube!"

Mike glanced at the man. The long white tube was leaning against the armrest next to him.

"It's long enough to hold a bat," said Mike. "But it might not be wide enough. I don't know if a bat would fit inside."

"I've got an idea," Kate said. "I saw a souvenir stand near the entrance. Let's go do an experiment!"

The Experiment

The souvenir stand stood in a corner by the main gate. Big circular racks of red and blue team shirts crowded the front entrance. Jerseys, balls, bobbleheads, and even Red Sox dog collars hung along the shop's back walls.

Bins of bats and racks filled with posters sat on the floor. Near the entrance stood a small glass checkout counter. The woman behind the cash register flipped through the pages of a travel magazine while a few customers looked at T-shirts.

The kids stopped at the pizza stand opposite the souvenir shop to make a plan.

"Let's split up. You go to the counter and keep the saleslady busy," said Kate. "I'll sneak in behind those racks of clothing. I want to check out the *bates de béisbol*."

Kate pointed to a bin of wooden bats in the back corner. The sign above the bin read BIG D'S BATTER'S BOX. OFFICIAL BATS JUST LIKE BIG D'S.

"I'm going to see if one of those bats fits inside a poster tube," Kate said. Near the bats was a rack filled with white tubes containing the Big D life-size posters. "Then we'll know if the man with the Yankees hat has the stolen bat hidden inside his tube. Just keep her busy, okay?"

Mike casually waved his hand at Kate. "No problem," he said. "I'm good at asking dumb questions."

When Mike got to the counter, the saleslady barely looked up from the glossy pictures of surfers and sandy beaches in the magazine in front of her. "Can I help you?" she mumbled.

Mike could tell that she didn't think a nine-year-old kid was an important customer.

"Umm, yeah," Mike replied. He watched Kate slip into the store and vanish behind a rack of clothes. He looked down at the small glass case. Inside were watches, baseballs, and other souvenirs. "I was wondering how much that thing is."

He pointed vaguely at a baseball in the case. Out of the corner of his eye, Mike saw Kate edge over to the rack of posters. She

picked one up and sneaked out of view.

"Well, it depends what you want," the saleslady said. She set her magazine aside. "What are you interested in?"

Mike pointed to the top shelf. "How about that?" he asked.

The saleslady picked up a pack of baseball cards.

"No, no, no . . . ," said Mike. "Not that. I want *thiiiiisssss*." He pointed to the baseball next to the cards.

The woman sighed. She took out the ball and handed it to Mike. He turned it over in his hands. The ball was covered with signatures of Red Sox players.

"Are these real?" he asked. Mike could tell they were just printed on the baseball. But he was trying to buy Kate some more time.

"Huh? No," said the saleslady. "The players didn't actually sign that ball. The signatures are just stamped on. A ball signed by all the Red Sox would cost more like eight hundred dollars, not eighteen dollars."

"Oh," Mike said, "I don't want it, then. Can I see that pen instead?"

The woman rolled her eyes and took the ball back from Mike. She returned it to the case and pulled out a brightly colored pen. It lit up red when a button was pushed.

Mike pushed the button over and over. The red light went on and off. The saleslady sighed again.

In the back of the store, Kate crouched next to the bin filled with replica Big D baseball bats. She glanced at the register. The saleslady was busy with Mike. Now was the perfect time.

Kate reached into the back of the bin and pulled out a bat.

Before it was halfway out, she realized the handle was speckled with sticky brown streaks. There were also scuff marks on the barrel of the bat.

"Yuck," she said. Kate put it back and wiped her hands on her pants. She didn't want to get the poster dirty. Quickly she picked another bat. The second bat was perfect, with a shiny wooden barrel and a clean handle.

Kate held it in her hand and popped off the end of the plastic poster tube. The poster was rolled tightly against the inside of the tube, leaving a big empty opening in the middle.

Kate slipped the bat into the tube. With a soft *whoosh,* it disappeared completely.

The bat fit perfectly inside the plastic poster tube!

Before anyone could see, Kate tipped the tube upside down, slid the bat out, and placed it back in the bin.

Up at the counter, Mike finished with the light-up pen. He paused for a moment and then asked to see a small wooden Red Sox bat.

The woman pulled out the bat and handed it to Mike. The top of the bat was painted red while the handle was wood-colored. Mike pretended to swing it. The saleslady didn't even crack a smile.

"I don't think you'll hit a home run with that," said Kate, coming up behind him. "Ready to go?"

"I guess so," Mike said. He set the bat down on the counter. "Thanks. I'm just not sure what I want. Maybe I'll come back later."

"Suit yourself," the woman said. She put the mini bat away and returned to her magazine.

Mike and Kate stopped next to the pizza stand.

"Did the bat fit?" Mike asked.

"Yes, perfectly," Kate said. "I think the man in the Yankees cap has Big D's bat inside his poster tube!"

"Wow!" said Mike. "But wouldn't people have seen him take it?"

"Not if they were all looking at Wally!" said Kate. "I'll bet he took the bat when everyone was watching Big D help Wally get up. He only needed a few seconds. He could have reached over the infield railing, grabbed the bat, and slipped it inside the poster tube. It's probably been right in front of us all this time!"

Big D at Bat

The second inning had just started. The Oakland A's were batting. They were already ahead by two runs, 2–0.

Loopy Lenfield, one of Boston's best pitchers, was on the mound. Loopy used his long fingers to throw knuckleball pitches that confused batters with weird dips and bobbles. When they worked, his knuckleballs were very hard to hit.

Mike and Kate slipped back into their

seats just as Boston made the second out of the inning.

One row in front of them, the man in the Yankees hat was watching the game along with all the other fans. Now a little boy sat next to him.

Kate elbowed Mike in the ribs. "See? The poster tube is still next to his seat," she whispered. "Who's that kid with him?"

"His grandson?" Mike guessed. "But maybe he's a decoy. Who would arrest a grandfather and his grandson?"

Kate twirled the end of her ponytail around her finger. She looked doubtful. "I don't know," she said. "Let's keep our eyes on that poster tube."

"Okay, but I want to see the game, too," Mike agreed. "We can hang here, watch the game, and wait for *him* to make a move."

On the field, Boston's first baseman caught a pop fly for the last out. The Athletics left their dugout and ran onto the field. Boston's players got ready to hit.

"Now batting for Boston," boomed the announcer, "Corky Collllllinnnnnns!"

Everyone cheered as Boston's center fielder, Corky Collins, stepped to the plate. Oakland's pitcher went into his windup. He let a fastball fly.

Corky swung around on his heels. He stretched his arms and the bat out as far as he could to reach the pitch. He hit it perfectly.

POW!

The ball took off, and so did the Athletics' right fielder. Just as the ball was about to clear the outfield wall, he jumped up and pulled it out of the air. The white ball stayed cradled at the top of his glove.

The crowd roared. Corky Collins was robbed of a home run!

"Bummer!" said Mike. "But what a cool catch! That's called a snow cone catch. The ball stays at the top of the glove, like a snow cone. Get it—a cool catch?"

Kate groaned and rolled her eyes.

The crowd cheered again. Boston's number two hitter was up. One more batter and it would be Big D's turn.

Three pitches later, the Boston batter headed back to the dugout. He had struck out. Oakland was having a good day. But the Boston fans weren't worried.

"Big D, Big D, Big D . . . ," the crowd chanted. A huge cheer went up when Big D came to the plate. It was so loud that Kate and Mike could barely hear the announcer.

Big D wasn't smiling as he usually did.

He also wasn't carrying his lucky bat. Instead, he held a dark brown bat. He stood next to the plate to test it.

"Oh no," said Mike. "Big D took six practice swings. Usually he only takes three. He must not be happy with that bat."

"Gee, Mike," Kate said. "How do you *know* these things?"

Mike shrugged.

The pitcher hurled the ball toward the home plate. It came in high and fast.

Swish! All that Big D's bat hit was air.

The pitcher wound up again and threw. It looked like another good pitch. Big D swung a second time.

Nothing! The Boston fans really wanted him to hit a home run. Could he do it without his lucky bat?

Big D dug his foot into the dirt. He took a

few more practice swings and waited for the next pitch.

The ball sailed over the plate. Big D swung. His bat connected with a powerful *THUNK*.

"Come on. Come on. Come on!" shouted Mike.

The ball zoomed almost straight up. The catcher tore off his mask. He backed up a few feet and positioned himself under the ball as it fell.

"Drop it! Drop it!" Mike shouted.

PLUNK! The ball landed right in the catcher's glove. Big D had popped out.

"Rats," Mike said, slapping his knee. "We needed a run."

The inning was over. Big D shuffled back to the dugout and tossed his bat to Bobby the batboy.

During Big D's turn at bat, Kate had also kept an eye on the man in the Yankees hat. She grabbed her cousin's arm. "Mike, look!" she exclaimed.

The man was reaching for the poster tube.

He handed the long white tube to the boy.

The boy, who looked about six, grabbed the tube excitedly. He gave the man a huge hug. Mike and Kate leaned forward to eavesdrop.

"How'd you know I wanted one of these, Grandpa Kevin?" the boy asked.

"I may be a Yankees fan, Nathan, but I know you love the Red Sox and Big D," said Grandpa Kevin. "I thought it would look great in your bedroom."

"I can't wait to hang it up," Nathan said.

"Well, before you do that, you may want to see what else is inside the tube," Grandpa Kevin said.

Nathan popped the cap off the end of the tube and tried to look inside. "It's too dark," he said. "What's in there?"

Nathan's grandfather smiled. He reached

over and tilted the bottom of the tube up. A tan blur slid out of the tube into Nathan's waiting hands.

Mike and Kate gasped.

It was Big D's Green Monster bat!

A Clue

Mike and Kate had found the stolen bat!

Nathan put the poster down and held the bat up to look at it from end to end. The wood of the barrel was polished and shiny. The bat almost seemed too heavy for the little boy to hold.

Kate leaned back in her seat and shook her head. "That's not the stolen bat," she declared.

"What?" Mike asked. "It sure looks like Big D's bat."

"It also looks brand-new. There isn't a nick or scuff mark anywhere on it," Kate said to Mike. "Big D's Green Monster bat would look used, not new. It's just a souvenir bat."

Mike studied the bat for a minute. Kate had a point. There was no way that Big D's favorite bat would be so clean.

"Okay, so we were wrong," he whispered. "I really thought that Grandpa Kevin might have stolen the bat."

Suddenly, the crowd booed loudly. Boston had missed an easy catch and Oakland scored again. It was 3–0, Oakland.

"Nope, but maybe he saw something during batting practice," Kate said. "Bobby said he was near the railing when Big D was signing autographs. Let's ask."

Mike nodded. "Sure," he said.

Mike cleared his throat loudly. "Ahem. Ah,

excuse me, sir," he said in a friendly voice.

Grandpa Kevin glanced back at Mike. "Oh, it's you," he said with a smile. "Need any sunflower seeds? I still have some left."

"No, thanks," Mike said, blushing. "I was just wondering about that bat. It looks like Big D's bat. The one that was stolen—"

"Stolen?" Nathan interrupted. "Big D's bat was stolen?"

"Uh-huh," said Mike. "Someone took it just after batting practice. He's using a different bat, but it's not working very well."

"Let me go give him this one, Grandpa!" said Nathan. "Maybe it'll help!"

"I don't know if that's a good idea," said Grandpa Kevin. "They probably have a rule against that."

"But he might want it," Nathan said. "Can I try, please?"

"Okay, okay," Grandpa Kevin said, smiling. "Go down to the railing and see if the batboy will bring your bat to Big D. But don't be surprised if he says no."

The three watched Nathan hurry toward the field. He waved to get Bobby's attention.

Mike turned back to Grandpa Kevin. "Were you near the dugout when Big D's bat was stolen?" he asked.

"I don't think so," Grandpa Kevin said. "I *was* standing by the railing during batting practice. I wanted to get the poster signed before the game, so I could surprise Nathan. But I didn't see anything suspicious. Big D's bat was right in front of me on the other side of the infield wall. I could have reached over and touched it if I wanted."

Kate's eyes opened wide. "Did you see anyone take the bat?" she asked.

"No." Grandpa Kevin laughed. "I guess I'd be talking to the police if I did. All I saw was Big D signing autographs, Wally, and the photographer."

"Oh yeah, we saw the photographer, too," said Mike. "Do you think maybe he took the bat?"

"I don't know," Grandpa Kevin said, pausing to think. "He seemed pretty nice. He told me he's been following Big D for weeks, taking pictures of him."

"Were you there when Wally tripped?" Kate asked.

"Yes. But I left right after that," said Grandpa Kevin. "I figured Big D was done signing autographs, and I went to meet my grandson at the main gate. He was late, so I stopped by the souvenir stand and bought the bat while I was waiting."

"Hey, look!" Mike said, pointing toward the field.

Nathan was still talking to Bobby, but Bobby was holding the new bat in his hands.

"Well, how about that?" Grandpa Kevin said. "It looks like Big D might use Nathan's bat after all! Maybe it'll help. The Red Sox could certainly use the runs."

Mike and Kate sat back in their seats.

Mike pulled the tennis ball from his jacket and started tossing it in the air. "It doesn't look good," he said to Kate.

"I know," replied Kate. "I don't have any other ideas of where that stolen bat might be."

"I'm not talking about the stolen bat," said Mike. "I'm talking about the game! We already have two outs. Big D isn't going to hit this inning unless the next guy gets on base."

The past few innings hadn't gone well for Boston. The score was still 3–0. With just a couple of innings left, the Red Sox needed to score soon or they'd lose.

Boston's next batter swung at the first pitch and hit a long, high foul ball. Mike and Kate jumped to their feet to try to catch it. It flew past them, but it was too high to reach. The batter stood at the plate as the next two pitches slid by.

"Ball one!" the umpire yelled after the first pitch.

"Ball two!" the umpire yelled after the second.

Mike stood up with the rest of the crowd. He stamped his feet, clapped, and chanted, "Home run. Home run. Home run."

While the crowd waited for the pitcher to throw, Kate noticed the photographer scouting out good shots. He was wearing the same jacket with big pockets that they had seen in the pressroom. The photographer snapped shots of all the fans standing and cheering.

Oakland's pitcher threw again. It was a high fastball over the center of the plate. Taking a small step forward with his left foot, the batter swung the bat around in a long, smooth sweep.

POW!

The hit sounded like a cannon going off. Oakland's center fielder raced to his right to catch the ball. It wasn't going to be easy. The ball flew over his head and dropped into the grass.

The center fielder scooped it up, but he bobbled it. The batter blew past first and charged for second. The center fielder got control of the ball and fired it off to second.

The runner reached his arms out and dove toward the base. At the same time, the second baseman caught the ball. He stretched out his glove to tag the runner.

The second-base umpire made a fist with his right hand and yanked it up into the air.

"YOU'RE OUT!" he yelled.

Thousands of boos rained down on the

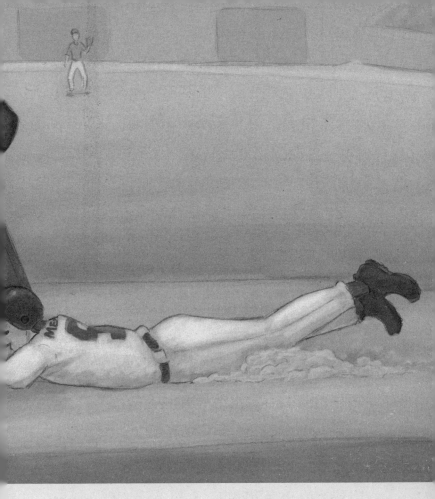

umpire. The runner stood up. He brushed off the dirt and jogged back to the Boston dugout. The Athletics trotted off the field. Now it was their turn to bat.

One of the Athletics' best hitters was up. He stood on deck taking practice swings. In between, he rested the bat on the ground.

Kate studied the bat. Although it looked like a new bat, its handle was covered with dark streaks.

Suddenly, she felt a gentle tap on her knee.

It was Grandpa Kevin. "I just thought of something else," he said. "When I went back to the souvenir stand to buy the bat, I bumped into the photographer. He was pretty friendly with the saleslady there. I didn't think much about it at the time. But if you think he took the bat . . ." Grandpa Kevin shrugged.

"That sounds like it might be a clue," said Kate. "Thanks for telling us."

Grandpa Kevin went back to watching the game.

Mike turned to Kate. "That's it! I think the photographer did it," he whispered. "We saw him in the pressroom just after the bat was stolen. Remember? I'll bet he stole the bat, put it in the tripod case, and dropped it off in the pressroom!"

Kate nodded along, then frowned. Her forehead wrinkled in concentration. "But why would he stop at the souvenir stand?" she asked.

Mike knew that Kate was always trying to figure out *why* something happened the way it did. He was usually just trying to *make* things happen.

"The saleslady could be in on it, too," said Mike. "She was reading a travel magazine when I was there. Maybe they're planning a big getaway! Let's go check it out!"

A Sticky Situation

Mike and Kate ran back to the souvenir stand. A little girl stood at the counter. She was buying the autographed baseball that Mike had looked at earlier.

When the girl walked away, Kate asked to see the small Red Sox bat in the case. The saleslady handed it to her.

"Let me know if you'd like to buy it, honey," the saleslady said. She looked down at her magazine. Kate stood on her tiptoes.

She tried to see if anything was hidden behind the counter.

While Kate snooped, Mike's eyes were drawn to the large TV hanging from the ceiling. Loopy Lenfield had just struck out three Athletics hitters in a row. The first half of the eighth inning was over. Boston would have only two more innings to score some runs.

The saleslady looked up at Kate. Kate put the small red bat back on the counter. Then she noticed the other items clustered around the register, including a jar of Red Sox pencils and pens, some Red Sox toothbrushes, and small bottles of Rawlings Liquid Pine Tar.

Kate picked up a bottle of pine tar. "What's this?" she asked Mike.

"It's sap, from a pine tree. It's sticky.

Players rub it on the handle of a bat to make it easier to grip," said Mike. "It keeps the bat from slipping out of your hands when you swing hard."

Kate nodded. She put the bottle down and studied the miniature Red Sox bat that was still lying on the counter.

"Sticky. It makes the bats sticky," Kate muttered to herself. She seemed lost in thought.

In front of them, the saleslady twirled a pencil in her right hand.

"Thanks for helping me," Kate said to her. "I'll come back later after I decide."

The saleslady nodded without even looking up.

Kate pulled Mike with her toward the back of the store. "Mike," she whispered, "pine tar makes bats sticky!"

"Yeah," he said, still distracted by the TV. "And water makes you wet. You've really learned a lot lately, haven't you?"

"Yes, if you want to know, I have," said Kate with a smile. "In fact, I just learned something important. I found out where the bat is. Want to see it?"

Mike's jaw dropped. What was Kate talking about? Before he could ask, she took off for the racks on the far wall.

Mike hustled to join Kate at the back of the store. She browsed through racks of red and blue Red Sox T-shirts.

"What are you doing?" he said, confused. "Are you buying a shirt? What about the bat?"

"No, I'm not buying a shirt," she answered. "I wanted to have an excuse to look in the back of the shop."

Kate ducked behind the racks of posters

and stood in front of the bin of replica Big D Green Monster bats.

Mike looked at the front counter. A noisy group of high school students had come into the shop and were throwing a foam baseball around. The saleslady was trying to get them to stop.

Kate sifted through the bats. After a few seconds, she found what she was looking for and pulled out one of the bats.

"That looks just like the one that Grandpa Kevin gave his grandson," Mike said.

"No, it doesn't," Kate said. She held out the handle. "Here, feel this."

Mike touched the handle of the bat. It was sticky. It felt like someone had eaten a sloppy peanut-butter-and-jelly sandwich and left fingerprints all over the bat.

Suddenly, the pieces fell into place.

GREEN MONSTER

"Pine tar," he said. "It's Big D's bat!"

"Exactly," Kate said.

"But if it's the real bat, why is it sitting here in this bin in the souvenir shop?" Mike asked.

"It's just like what the Yawkeys did with their initials on the scoreboard. Someone hid it in plain sight!" said Kate. "Why would anyone think it was the real bat? I saw it earlier and didn't think of it. And who would want to buy a dirty bat when they can have a clean one? It was perfectly safe here!"

The saleslady was ringing up purchases for a few of the high school students. She wasn't paying attention to Kate and Mike.

Kate went on. "I'll bet the photographer stole the bat when Wally tripped. He brought it up here to hide it so the security guards wouldn't find it on him if they searched him."

"Wow!" Mike said. "We need to let someone know! Should we buy it and turn it in?"

Kate looked at the price tag and shook her head. "We don't have enough money," she said. "But I have an idea. . . ."

Kate took a Red Sox T-shirt and covered the sticky bat with it. Making sure that the saleslady wasn't watching, Kate popped open the end of one of the poster tubes and slipped the stolen bat inside. Then she slid the tube *under* the poster rack.

"That should keep it safe from the thief. Boy, will he be surprised if he comes back and the bat is gone!" she said.

"Let's go tell Bobby," Mike said.

The two raced back through the ballpark. There was a deafening roar as they reached the top of the aisle leading down to Boston's dugout.

Almost all the fans were cheering. With one runner on base, the Red Sox batter had just nailed a long shot out to right field. The right fielder missed the ball and then bobbled the throw. That left Red Sox players on second and third with no outs. Maybe Boston finally had a chance.

As the fans settled down, Mike and Kate scanned the field for Bobby. Mike spotted him crouched near the Red Sox dugout. Big D would be up next.

Mike and Kate hurried to the infield wall.

"Pssst," Kate whispered. "Bobby."

Bobby turned around to see Kate and Mike on the other side of the wall. "What's up?" he asked.

"We've got some big news," said Kate. She motioned for him to come closer.

Bobby slid over against the wall. He tilted his head back a little so he could listen to Kate as she whispered. He kept his eyes on the game the whole time.

Kate told him the entire story about the bat in the souvenir stand and what they thought the photographer had done.

"Wow, that's amazing!" Bobby said.

While they were talking, the Boston batter had hit a single down the third-base line and made it to first. Finally—three men on base for the Red Sox and Big D was up. Boston could pull ahead if Big D hit a home run.

"I'll be right back," Bobby told Kate and Mike. "Don't go anywhere!"

Bobby ran to the dugout and brought out the new bat that Nathan had given Big D earlier. Bobby rubbed a little pine tar on the clean handle and whispered something into Big D's ear.

Big D's face broke into a big smile. He took the bat, swung three practice swings, and stepped into the batter's box.

Bobby gave Kate and Mike a thumbs-up sign.

The Athletics' pitcher threw the ball low and inside.

POW!

The ball blasted off the end of Big D's bat. It lifted up over the shortstop's head. It flew high over the left fielder's head. And it sailed far over the Green Monster.

A grand slam for Big D! One runner after another scored as Big D circled the bases. He stopped just before home plate and then jumped on it with both his feet. The entire team crowded around him. They gave him high fives and slapped him on the back. Boston was winning for the first time in the game!

Big D tipped his hat once to the crowd. He picked up the bat he had borrowed from Nathan. With a wide smile, he held the bat up in the air and gave it a big kiss!

The MVPs

Kate and Mike stood against the infield railing near the Red Sox dugout and watched Fenway Park empty out.

"What an amazing game!" Kate said. "We got to sit right next to the Red Sox dugout, *and* we got to see them win!"

"Big D's grand slam was great," said Mike. "I can't believe the new bat worked!"

"Where do you think Bobby went?" asked Kate. "He said he'd come back to talk to us after the game. . . . Hey, there's my mom!"

"You two have been busy," Kate's mother said. She was walking down the aisle with a computer bag slung over her shoulder. A man and woman dressed in dark blue security uniforms were with her.

"I hear you kids are heroes!" said the first security guard. "My name is Dennis, and this is Tashia. We're in charge of security at the stadium."

"We just finished interviewing the photographer and the saleslady at the souvenir stand," Tashia said. "The saleslady didn't have anything to do with it. The photographer simply made friends with her and decided to hide the bat in the store. He was worried we might search his equipment."

"We're lucky you were paying attention," said Dennis. "Otherwise the photographer was going to go back to the souvenir stand, buy the bat, and leave. A private collector offered him lots of money for it."

"How did he get the bat from the field to the souvenir shop without anyone seeing it?" asked Mrs. Hopkins.

"The photographer had an empty tripod case," Dennis said. "When everyone was watching Big D help Wally, he slipped the bat into the case. Then he brought it to the souvenir shop the first chance he had. He knew they'd search the photographers' area and his equipment."

"He dropped off the tripod case in the pressroom to give him a reason to leave the field," said Tashia. "We found the stolen bat in the poster tube, where you kids put it. Thank you. And now I think Bobby has a surprise for you."

Kate and Mike turned back toward the field.

"Hi, guys," said Bobby. He was standing next to the Red Sox dugout. "I got special permission for you to visit the dugout."

"Wowee!" said Mike. "They usually don't let anyone in a dugout after a game!"

Bobby opened a small gate, and Kate and Mike stepped down onto the crunchy red infield dirt. Kate's mother and the two security officers followed.

"The field looks so much bigger when you're down here," Kate said. "I can't imagine hitting a home run all the way over that wall."

Kate was right. The field *did* seem bigger. Mike couldn't believe he was walking on the same grass that the Red Sox played on. It was like a dream come true.

Bobby led the group into the Red Sox dugout. Used paper cups were strewn all over the floor, and empty water bottles were stacked high in a recycling bin in the corner.

Mike and Kate watched the grounds crew clean up. They didn't notice that someone else had joined them in the dugout.

"How do you like the view?" asked a voice.

It was Big D!

Mike's jaw dropped open. Kate stared up at Big D's huge shoulders and wide smile.

"I hear you kids did something pretty special for me," Big D said. "That's why the Boston Red Sox wanted to do something special for you. Both of you."

He pulled his right hand from behind his back, held out a baseball, and dropped it into Mike's hand.

It was a brand-new major-league baseball. It looked just like any other major-league baseball, except for one thing.

Mike's eyes grew wide.

"Hey, this is autographed by all the Red Sox players!" he said. "Thanks, Big D!"

Big D nodded. "You're welcome. It's nice to have my bat back," he said. "Now, I have something for you as well, young lady." He brought his left hand from behind his back.

In it was Big D's Green Monster bat!

"I'm afraid that I can't give you the real one," said Big D. "But this one is just like it."

Kate lifted the bat from Big D's outstretched hands. Mike leaned closer and watched her twirl the bat around. There was a message from Big D written in black marker along the barrel of the bat.

My two favorite MVPs—Mike and Kate. Next time I hit a home run, it's for you. Big D.

BALL-PARK
Mysteries 1

Dugout Notes
☆ Fenway Park ☆

Knuckleballs. The knuckleball pitcher Loopy Lenfield doesn't exist, but knuckleballs do. They are actually thrown with the pitcher's fingertips, not his or her knuckles.

The Green Monster. Fenway's famous left-field wall really is a monster. It's a thirty-seven-foot-high wall, the tallest in baseball. It has a huge effect on the games at Fenway. Line drives that might be home runs in other baseball parks simply bounce off the Green Monster. But since the wall is close to home plate (310 feet), high, short fly balls that might be caught for an out in other parks can become home runs at Fenway. The Green Monster was originally made of wood. Later it was covered in tin and concrete. Today it's covered in hard plastic. The wall used to be plastered with advertisements. The ads were painted over in 1947. They were too distracting for hitters.

A second home. Although it's the oldest major-league ballpark, Fenway Park is actually the second home for the Red Sox. The Red Sox were first known as the Boston Americans. The Boston Americans were one of the original members of the American League in 1901. Before Fenway Park opened in 1912, they played at the Huntington Avenue Grounds. Fenway Park got its name because it's in the Fenway section of Boston.

A gift from Dad. Charles Taylor was a Civil War veteran and owner of the *Boston Globe* newspaper. It would be nice to have a dad like him. He bought the Red

Sox for his son, John Taylor, in 1904. Charles Taylor picked the name Red Sox in 1907 and changed the uniform to include red stockings in 1908.

Wally. Wally is the Red Sox mascot. He's a large green monster, like the left-field wall, the Green Monster.

The monster and the cliff. In the beginning, the Green Monster wasn't alone. From 1912 to 1933, a steep ten-foot hill ran in front of the wall from the left-field foul pole to the old flag-pole in center field. That meant playing left field at Fenway Park wasn't easy. Left fielders often spent most of the game running uphill to catch balls. The Red Sox left fielder Duffy Lewis was so good at playing balls along the hill that the area became known as Duffy's Cliff. In 1934, a large part of Fenway Park burned, including the Green Monster. When the team rebuilt the stadium, it removed the cliff.

Green Monster seats. In 2003, the Red Sox added new seats on top of the Green Monster.

A large scoreboard. These days, most ballparks have electronic scoreboards. Not Fenway Park. Fenway still has a hand-operated scoreboard. It's one of the last in the major leagues. During games, people sit inside the wall and post the score with large, three-pound numbers. Each number is sixteen inches square.

Still waiting for a home run. It's hard to hit a home run over the Green Monster. But it's even harder to clear the right-field roof. No one has hit a home run over Fenway's right-field roof yet. It's just too far away.

Read on for the beginning of
the next Ballpark Mysteries book,

The Pinstripe Ghost

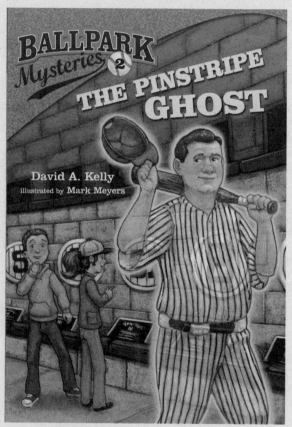

BALLPARK
Mysteries 2
THE PINSTRIPE
GHOST

David A. Kelly
illustrated by Mark Meyers

Mike Walsh had always wanted to visit Yankee Stadium. But now that he was there, he just wanted to leave.

"When do you think this will be over?" he asked his cousin Kate Hopkins. The two were sitting in the back row of a press conference at the stadium. "I can't wait to try out that rooftop pool at the hotel!"

"Soon. You know my mom—super sports reporter!" Kate said. She pulled her long brown ponytail through the back of a blue Cooperstown baseball cap. "She always likes to stay until the end and get in one last question."

"Just like you," Mike teased.

Kate's mother was a reporter for the website American Sportz. She and the kids were at Yankee Stadium in New York City for a spring weekend series against the Seattle Mariners. They had driven down Friday morning from their home in upstate New York.

At the front of the room, a team official was talking about the upcoming series. The first Mariners–Yankees game was the next day.

Mike drummed his fingers on the side of his chair. He liked action more than talk. And press conferences were *all* talk and *no* action. But at least it was baseball talk.

The official finished answering a question. "That's it for today," he said. "Except for one thing. The famous author Mr. Robert Williams will be here all weekend near the main entrance. He'll be signing copies of his new book, *Ghosts in the Ballpark: A History of Haunted Baseball Stadiums and Supernatural Superstars.*"

"What about the ghost of Babe Ruth?"

Mrs. Hopkins asked. "Will he show up this weekend?"

Kate turned to Mike, her brown eyes wide. "A ghost?" she asked. "How come Mom didn't tell us about it?"

"Aunt Laura probably wanted it to be a surprise," Mike replied. Suddenly, he wasn't bored at all. "*Shh.* I want to hear what he says."

"Ummmm . . . I—I don't know," the man stammered. He mopped his brow and riffled through his papers. Mike thought he looked like he was stalling for time. "Officially, there aren't any ghosts in Yankee Stadium."

"Some people are saying that the stadium is haunted," Mrs. Hopkins added, "because the original Yankee Stadium where Babe Ruth played was torn down and this new one was built."

A few of the other reporters nodded.

"I talked to some workers. They have heard strange noises," a reporter with long blond hair put in.

"Oh, noises," the official said. He waved a hand. "Yankee Stadium is big. You'll always have some funny noises here and there. But those stories about a ghost are just that—stories." He gave a nervous laugh.

"So you have no comment about Babe Ruth's ghost?" Mrs. Hopkins asked. "Or if he'll be here this weekend?"

"No," the official said. "Leave the questions about supernatural superstars to Mr. Williams. He's the expert. We'll focus on baseball."

Mike had never heard anything so cool. He leaned toward Kate. "Let's try to find the ghost!" he said.